I'm so Fat

Sandra Lorange

authorHOUSE®

AuthorHouse™
1663 Liberty Drive, Suite 200
Bloomington, IN 47403
www.authorhouse.com
Phone: 1-800-839-8640

First published by AuthorHouse 1/2/2008

ISBN: 978-1-4343-5231-6 (sc)

Printed in the United States of America
Bloomington, Indiana

This book is printed on acid-free paper.

August 8, 2004

I'm spinning out of control. I don't know when it all started. The only thing I know for sure is that I am out of control. I am starving all the time and tortured with thoughts about food. My stomach has hunger pains morning, noon, and night. The pain pierces my stomach like a cramp; pinching, gnawing, tightening. I think about food all the time; I'm just so afraid to eat. Yuck, the thought of food makes me so unhappy. I'm so fat.

August 15, 2004

I don't remember how I began to lose the weight. I turned thirteen a month ago, on July 15. I weighed myself on my birthday and I was 150 pounds. Now, a month later, I weigh 130 pounds. No one would notice. The reason is I'm so fat.

August 17, 2004

I've been at the same elementary school for seven years. Suddenly my parents are making me go to another school this fall, called Bentley Junior High. I had no say in the matter. My parents just told me I would be going to another school, and that's that. No discussion. All my girlfriends will be at a different school than me and I hate it. My parents won't even listen to me. They listen with the "aha, aha" and then make a totally different decision without considering what I think or feel. It's just the way it is. You can see right through them, they are so transparent.

They pretend to listen, but they ignore me. Listening is a big hassle for them. We have these debates that go nowhere 'cause in the end, I know they will do what they want anyway. There's no democracy in my house. My parents don't even see how miserable everyone is around this house. They pretend. They are the best at pretending; it's a science. First-place winners every time. The gold medal goes to … Marty Dee's parents, for knowing it all.

August 20, 2004

I bought some new clothes for school today. A few cropped tops and a pair of low-rise jeans. Big deal. I look disgusting in all of them. I bulge out everywhere. When I got home, I weighed myself and I am 125 pounds. The shirts look too tight and my fat hangs over the top of the pants at my waist. I'm so fat.

August 23, 2004

It's so amazing. Really, when you think about how no one notices me. I get away with not eating. We don't eat together. Our family never spends mealtime together, so they don't see me eat anyway. I finally realized how well losing weight is working for me. My parents are busy, either out working late or just not home during mealtime. Wow! I am getting away with it. I can starve myself and no one catches me. My brother and sister don't know either. I lost two more pounds.

September 6, 2004

I hate the walk to school, the kids, everything. It takes
about fifteen minutes to walk to school. Like I said, all
my close girlfriends go to a different junior high school
in another part of the city. Winnipeg is not a big city, but
it sure seems huge when your friends go to a different
school. I wish my parents allowed me to be with my
friends. I'm sick of hearing "you're not allowed" every time
I say I want to do something. It would make school a
whole lot better. I miss my friends. It sucks to be me.

September 15, 2004

I walk to my locker alone and no one talks to me. I walk
to and from school alone. I stand by myself in front of my
locker, and no one talks to me. I am alone all the time. I
am so lonely.
When you look at me from the outside, I'm just an
ordinary kid. I wear low-rise tight blue jeans, flared at
the bottom. I wear hoodies and cute t-shirts with sayings
on the front. I love to wear colored plastic bracelets and
silver rings on my fingers, like the stuff you buy at Claire's.
My hair, long and curly, hangs halfway down my back. I
straighten it with a flat iron. During the summer, I dyed
it blue, my favorite color. The dye is fading now. I love to
wear dark black nail polish. The last week before school
started, I pierced my belly button. There is a beautiful blue
ball called "lapis lazuli" in it.

September 20, 2004

School is easy for me, real easy. As a matter of fact, I am a
bit of a perfectionist when it comes to my schoolwork, and
have extremely high marks. I never get under 90 percent
on school assignments. My parents think as long as my
marks are good, everything is fine. Schoolwork is not
difficult for me; it's everything else I worry about. I love
to play in the band. I play all the percussion instruments.
I listen to music like Green Day and Good Charlotte. My
parents monitor the music I listen to. Can you believe they
truly believe I don't listen to the music they ban? I sneak
behind their backs.
I stepped on the scale in my parents' bathroom, and I saw
that I lost six more pounds.

September 22, 2004

This weekend, we went to close up our cottage at
Whispering Pines Lake. It is about two hours from the
city. The lake is lonely, too. There is no one my age up
there, and it is boring. It used to be one of my favorite
places. I spent hours swimming and exploring along the
shore, feeling carefree. Summer vacation seems like eons
ago.

September 23, 2004

I think about gaining weight all the time. I think about it
so much, it has taken over all my thoughts. I have a voice

in my head that keeps telling me I have to be thin. I lost
four more pounds this week.

My friends I have know since grade one in elementary
school, Sarah, Dianne, and Genevieve, told me how thin I
looked. "Wow, Marty," they said, "Do you ever look great!"
But they're not telling me the truth, because I know I am
fat.

Starving yourself makes you feel pain all over your body.
And you wonder how someone can do that to themselves
but once you're in, it's easy.

October 3, 2004

Feeling hungry is better than my other feelings. The pain
gnaws away at my body, so my brain is numb to the other
thoughts in my head. My life is a mess. I feel terrible and
lonely. Then, the next minute, my thoughts torment me.
The loneliness is like an eerie void. It feels like when you
jump in the lake and for a moment you are suspended
under the water. A void fills in around you unlike anything
above the water. The water creates another place. You
are suspended in another world. My loneliness feels the
same way. Starving feels better than the emptiness. I need
someone to help me.

October 5, 2004

My soul aches. I never thought it would hurt this much to
stop eating. The whole thing is out of control now.

… I can't stop what's happening to me. I lost more weight again. I weigh myself every chance I get. Time passes so slowly in my head, but the scale says the weight is coming off quickly now. I won't stick anything in my mouth unless I know how many calories it has. Thoughts of food are in my head all the time. It is torturing me. It's all I think about. I am obsessed with thoughts of food. I am obsessed with how to avoid eating. I am obsessed with food. I am starving. I have pain in my body all the time.

When I'm hungry, it is so painful. So sometimes I eat a bit and then put my finger down my throat. At first it was gross, but then I got so I could do it without a gagging sound. This works even better. I lost four pounds this week.

October 6, 2004

My stomach hurts and cramps. My throat is swollen and raw from throwing up food. The hunger pains are horrible, but it's better than being fat. I am hungry every minute of every day. I only lost one pound.

I am going to starve myself to death. It's not easy anymore. I crave thinness. I am successful at it. My friend Sarah told me I am moody these days. She noticed how thin my face is.

I went to the locker room in the gym to look in the mirror before gym class today. I feel half-dead. Exercise is good to burn calories. Hopefully I will be thinner soon.

October 10, 2004

I weighed myself this morning before going to school, and I weigh 106 pounds. I was able to get out of the house without eating a thing. My parents had gone to work early.

October 11, 2004

It's getting trickier to not eat. My parents suspect something is up.

Last night, my dad was asking my mom if she thought I was too thin. My dad thinks something is up. This is what I overheard him saying about me, "Marty Dee has lost so much weight that her face has changed. The skin on her face looks sallow and grey. Her eyes have begun to sink into the sockets in her skull, and are dull and hollow. Her face looks shrunken and her skin is like white glue pasted to her bones. She is starting to look like a skeleton. She is distant and aloof. I am worried about her."

October 13, 2004

I was fat all my life, even when I was a little kid. I was looking through photos today for a school assignment, and I looked disgusting. My shirts stopped in mid-belly, and my fat hung down below between my shirt and my pants. Nothing looked nice. I hated myself in every picture. I looked like a fat blob. I hated myself in all the pictures with my stomach sticking out and my jeans so tight. I look fat. I hate the way I looked then, and I hate the way I look now. I am so fat.

October 14, 2004

Now, even when I try to eat, my stomach cramps so badly,
I want to cry. The pain pierces my stomach, and I reject
the food. My stomach flips and flops inside. At school
today, I asked to be excused to go to the washroom to
throw up after lunch, because I didn't want anyone to
catch me. I am so quick that I can spit up in the garbage
can without making a sound, and get back to class without
being caught. No one suspects anything. If no one is
looking, I can quickly and silently spit into any garbage
can, anytime, anywhere. I am so messed up.
I weigh 106 pounds today. There is a voice inside me
telling me I am fat. I feel so empty inside.

October 23, 2004

I seem to do a lot of crying these days. My dad is traveling
to the States to work for ten days, and I miss him so
much when he's away. He has traveled for as long as I can
remember. I mean, I know he's coming back, he always
does, but it's just that our house is so empty without him.

November 3, 2004

My dad arrived home from his trip today, he took one look
at me and it was straight to the hospital. His suspicions
were validated, there was no denying it, something was
drastically wrong. At the hospital I was diagnosed with
an eating disorder called anorexia nervosa. I have lost too

much weight. Since my dad left on October 23, I have lost ten pounds. I have lost forty-four pounds in four months. The doctor told my dad that my weight is down below my ideal body weight. I should weigh about 118 pounds and I am already 12 pounds below that.

November 5, 2004

The worst thing now is that people stare at me. I don't know what they see. When I look in a mirror, I hate what I see. My aunt once said my eyes are the window to my soul. Looking into my eyes, all you see is darkness. I have darkness all around me. My head is full of dark thoughts about death. When you look into a sick person's eyes, you can see sickness, emptiness. It stares back at you.

November 6, 2004

My stomach pain lets me know I am still alive, even though I wish I were dead. The rest of me feels nothing. I wonder if death feels like this. My parents always tell me I have it so good. Life is heavenly. All I see is darkness.

November 7, 2004

The doctor said I have an eating disorder. The clinic in the hospital "specializes" in dealing with disorders like anorexia nervosa and anorexia bulimia. The clinic offers "a family approach" in order to get me back on track. They want families to nurture the member with the eating disorder back to health. They are trying to "retrain me" to have healthy and nutritious eating habits.

November 8, 2004

We had a meeting, and the doctors told the whole family what was going on with me. We meet at the clinic in the hospital, and we have family therapy once a week on Tuesday mornings. I go separately for counseling on Thursdays. There is a team of people who are trying to help me. We meet, they talk, they weigh me, and they talk some more. The talking is mostly for my parents; psychological stuff. I don't listen, but I guess it helps them. I don't care what they think; I am fat.

This is what happens: I meet with different people. There is a social worker, a nurse, my own doctor, and a psychiatrist.

In therapy on Thursday, they told me that once you have no fat left in your body, the body begins to eat itself, and you lose all your muscles. Muscles are protein. When you starve yourself, eventually your body begins to metabolize its own protein for energy. If this is not corrected— death—you die.

The doctors are afraid that I will have a heart attack, or what they call cardiac arrest. My heart is a muscle, and muscles are made of protein. My heart is being damaged by the eating disorder.

All of my organs are in trouble, and my hormones are out of whack. I don't get my period anymore.

November 9, 2004

The doctors explained anorexia to me. We have discussions about my anxiety surrounding meals, food, calories. My family thinks I am difficult and moody. Being moody is the understatement of the century. I fight my parents on each and every food particle that enters my mouth. I refuse to eat food that makes me fat. I don't listen to all their talk. I am not interested in what they have to say. It's like a conspiracy, and everyone keeps telling me I am thin, but I am fat.

November 14, 2004

My real fear is the fear of gaining weight. I need to control it. I have to control my weight. It sounds bizarre, but I am afraid to gain any weight back.

November 16, 2004

Clearly, I have been told by the doctor that I am underweight. I weigh ninety-six pounds. I am so close to death and have absolutely been told that I could die of cardiac arrest and yet I keep trying to stop myself from eating. My fear of gaining weight is so intense that I cannot see the thinness everyone talks to me about. I am unable to see how thin I am.

November 18, 2004

There are voices in my head telling me I am fat. My brain
and my feelings are all mixed up. My brain understands I
have an eating disorder, but my feelings tell me I'm fat. It
doesn't make sense.

Dylan, my brother, thinks I'm trying to get attention.
It's not true. I never thought my problem affected other
people. I really didn't.

My sister was really concerned when the doctors told her
I could die. I think that freaked her out. She found out
I weighed a hundred and two pounds and just said "Oh
my God" or something like that. I didn't mean to involve
everyone in my misery. I never really thought about how
all this would affect my family. I don't care what they think
now, because I feel no one really cares about me. I am the
one who is hurting. I am the one in pain.

November 19, 2004

The hospital visits are so boring. While I am in the
doctor's office, I read a pamphlet on how long it takes to
cure someone with anorexia. It is a long time, months and
months. Sometimes there is no cure and you die.

It will take months to put on the proper amount of
weight. If I lose more weight, I could actually die of a heart
attack. Can you believe it? It will be harder to put the
weight on than it was to take it off.

The clinic I go to uses a family approach. Everyone is
involved in my weight gain. They want me to relearn

healthy eating habits. I never had healthy eating habits. I am fat. The doctors suggested to my parents that it's better for me to gain the weight at home. Putting me in the hospital to overcome my anorexia is not as effective, as using a family approach. It's all going to be better at home. I don't know how they think this could be true.

November 20, 2004

Staying in the hospital with an intravenous tube feeding me calories would be gross. I hate needles. Gaining weight is gross too. It is torture at home. I'm afraid of everything. I'm afraid to gain weight. Doesn't anyone hear me? My parents don't hear me. When I speak, they don't look like they are hearing what I say. I scream and cry about eating. They make me eat anyway.

November 21, 2004

I would tell you this isn't a way to get attention, but you sure do get it. I have never spent so much time with my mom in my whole life; it's amazing. She is actually spending time with me and paying attention to me. Someone is with me all the time now, and I am never alone.

Everyone is concerned about me—my grandparents, my brother Dylan, and my sister, Natalie, my mom and dad, my friends. Everyone is trying to support me in this disease. It is hard because people don't know what to say. They don't know whether to be sympathetic or talk about the disease with me or not. They're afraid to talk about how I look 'cause it's such a big deal to me. I cry a lot because I am so fat.

November 24, 2004

Suddenly, I have too much attention. I got caught vomiting in the basement bathroom, and it all started to spiral out of control. My life has not been the same since. I am monitored all the time by watching eyes. I am barely functioning ... barely alive.

November 27, 2004

I am so tired. I can't meet my friends on Friday night, I can't focus in class, and I can't walk to school without being totally exhausted. I feel tired all the time and can barely walk up and down the stairs at home.
I can't concentrate on my schoolwork anymore. I can't do anything. My grades are dropping.
I am even too tired to talk on MSN with my girlfriends. I can't be bothered.

November 28, 2004

I feel like a prisoner. My parents follow me around and I have to pee with the bathroom door open so everyone can make sure I don't throw up any food after I eat. I am a prisoner. Can you imagine leaving the door open when you pee so your parents can check up on you? It is totally embarrassing. To make matters worse, Dylan and Natalie snitch on me too. They report when they see me spit into the garbage can in my room. They think it's gross when I spit in the garbage cans. They look at me with the weirdest looks, like I am strange. Everyone is a private eye around here. It's the "Anorexic Detective Agency" at your service.

December 1, 2004

Another thing that happens to you when you become anorexic is that you don't get your period anymore. The doctor calls it menses. A.K.A. the menstrual cycle.

December 2, 2004

I can't go to sleep on my own anymore. All kinds of things make me nervous. I feel scared all the time. Things like being out of control, and getting fat if I eat too much, and my dropping grades, and what people are thinking when they look at me. I need help. Maybe I need someone to understand. Someone who knows how I feel. The voices. The pain. The loneliness. I want to leap out of my skin. My dad lies with me at night until I fall asleep. My mom thinks I like myself, but she is really stupid. I hate myself. She just doesn't get it.

December 5, 2004

This disease sucks the life out of everyone. My parents and my brother and sister watch my every move. Everyone is on high alert. They follow me around and don't trust me. They make sure I don't puke in the garbage cans or the toilets. They follow me everywhere, and I have to leave the bathroom door open. Everyone is aware of my presence all the time. Now I know what a caged zoo animal feels like. Being watched 24-7 is hell.

The tension is horrible. Living in our home is like one big huge stress ball. Everyone is cranky and bitchy all the time. I wonder if it was like this before and I never noticed. Maybe everything wasn't fine … No one really talks … about how they feel around here … about what they feel. I am suffocating in emptiness. Can't anybody help me?

December 10, 2004

Our house doesn't feel good. I mean its feels totally empty. There is absolutely no Christmas spirit in our house. If I were writing a Dickens novel, this place would be Scrooge's house. I bet other homes have lots of Christmas spirit. Some people probably have laughter and fun. Not our place. We may have a huge tree with hundreds of expensive German glass ornaments, but who cares? What's the point of having things if no one is happy around here? Genevieve's parents have a real Charlie Brown tree that the kids pick out themselves, all decorated with homemade ornaments, and I think it's beautiful. Whenever I go to her house, I look at the tree with tiny mismatched lights and different-colored strands of garland, and I think to myself how nice their tree looks and how good their house makes me feel. I wonder if my home ever felt like that, even before I had anorexia. I wonder. I wonder about a lot of my feelings.

December 11, 2004

Counting calories is everything. It is a way of life, a negotiation, an existence.

I drink tea and low-calorie soft drinks because they have no calories. I don't want to get fat. I have to put on weight, but I am afraid.

My anorexia has been out in the open for a few months now. Finally they caught me this week at weigh-in time. I have been stuffing my bra with little lead weight pellets I found down in the basement in the workspace. I was trying to fool my parents and the doctor about how much weight I was gaining. Now when I weigh in, I have to wear a hospital gown with nothing underneath; they even make me go to the bathroom ahead of time, so my weight will be more accurate. I'm not a dishonest person, but the voice in my head tells me to lie. It's the disease talking. I, Marty Dee, don't lie. The disease lies.

December 12, 2004

Today, when I got home after school, I went straight to my room to look in the mirror, and there is no denying that I am fat. Some days I turn all the mirrors around backwards so I can't see myself. I don't want to see how fat I am. I even hum a song to myself to block out the voices,
"Look at me I'm Marty Dee,
I'm fat, as fat as fat can be."
Mirrors aren't my friends.

December 13, 2004

I have no energy to move around. I used to play soccer all year round. I am the keeper. My soccer coach knows how good I am in net, but now I can't play soccer at all because I am tired all the time and my legs hurt. I have no energy to do anything. It is even hard to climb the stairs to go to bed. I have to sit and rest partway up. It sucks to be me. My parents said no more sports until I'm healthy again. You can't erase soccer from my life just like that. It's so unfair. I have nothing now. I think the anorexia is just an excuse for my mom to say no soccer because she doesn't want to be bothered taking me to soccer anyway. Usually, when she drives, we are late arriving for the games and the other keeper starts the game. It must be a big inconvenience to her.

December 14, 2004

In the last couple of weeks, when I get home from school, I get on the running machine and exercise like a crazy maniac. My parents caught me doing this and now I am monitored for absolutely everything. My mom had to take me to a specialist at the sports medicine clinic, because there is something wrong with my legs. They referred me to a specialist. Here we go again with all the doctors. I went to see another doctor who is a pediatric neurosurgeon, because my legs are bothering me. My left leg doesn't respond properly. I can't move it properly, and my foot just hangs down. The doctor told my mom and dad that I have "drop foot." The nerve in my left leg is damaged. This has been caused by the anorexia.

December 15, 2004

What else can possibly happen to me? My life is pathetic enough as it is. I don't really need more problems. I feel like a freak. Sometimes I feel like I want to die.

December 17, 2004

Did you know that I started to grow fine hair all over my body? I noticed it on my stomach area and on my lower back, even on my face. I was staring at my face in the mirror before school today and saw it.

My body is growing hair because my body temperature is dropping. Since my body has little or no fat left, it can't keep my core temperature constant. My body is trying to keep warm, so it grows hair. My regular body temperature has dropped two degrees lower than my normal body temperature.

I feel too tired to care about how I look anymore. I already feel like a freak. I'm already odd; what's a little hair on your fat belly anyway?

December 18, 2004

The doctor says homeostasis is the body's regulatory state of equilibrium. Whenever something changes in the body, it tries to maintain itself. So basically, the body functions at a constant temperature. Sometimes the temperature goes up, like when you have an infection or the flu, and sometimes it drops, like when you get too cold. The body adapts to regulate and maintain its temperature.

December 19, 2004

I am always cold. The bones on my back stick out whenever I bend over. It's kinda gross. I have to wear at least two warm fleecy tops over my shirt to stay warm. I am never warm anymore. I sit with a blanket on me all the time. Winter temperatures don't help either. The more clothes I wear hide my body.

One good thing that has happened this week is that my parents let me change schools, because they thought it might make it better for me, so now I am back with my friends. My friends know about my anorexia and are trying to be supportive. At lunchtime, we all sit in the cafeteria and they make sure I eat.

December 20, 2004

I got my report card today, because it's the last day before school ends for winter break. My grades are dropping. My marks fell from ninety-six to eighty-six in most of my subjects. I guess I am not a perfectionist after all. I haven't been able to do gym for a while, but I can't concentrate on my other work either. The teachers all know about "my situation" and don't say much to me about missing class.

Christmas break might be fun. I'll be away from school. My friends and I can hang out, go shopping for clothes, and have sleepovers.

My parents have a ton of people in over the holidays, so they won't be watching me too carefully. I will get away with not eating much easier.

December 23, 2004

We went to visit my aunt and uncle. My aunt's house is fun. Her house is full of Christmas spirit. She has a Charlie Brown Christmas tree too, just like my friend Genevieve. The tree is five feet tall and terribly crooked at the top. The trunk bends out in the middle. It was full of little bits of bright twinkling lights that made you feel so good that all you want to do is sit and stare at the twinkling lights. I told my aunt how great it felt to be in her house, because there was NO Christmas spirit in my house.

December 25, 2004

I got some nice gifts for Christmas this year. I got clothes from Garage and Roxy. I even got a pair of workout pants from Lululemon.

It was hard not to eat at Christmas dinner, with all the festivity going on and the large amounts of food. I had to be very tricky. The house was full of people—my grandparents and aunts and uncles and friends of my parents.

I have to play head games and make eating a competition. The challenge is not to eat … if I am worthy, I can achieve the goal of getting through the day with eating as little food as possible, but if I give in to it (food), then I am weak, no good, and unworthy. I play the game with myself all the time.

After dinner, everyone treated me different. It weirded me out. We sat around in the living room, and my auntie sat and combed my hair and I got all kinds of attention. Maybe they feel sorry for me or something.

December 29, 2004

I am eating too much over the holidays and I am fat. Uugh. I can't weigh myself at home, because my dad hid the bathroom scale. I am only allowed to weigh myself once a week at the doctor's office. I am struggling to stay thin.

January 4, 2005

I am back at school. I am afraid all the time about just about anything, so I call my dad. Lunchtime is particularly a bad time for me because of the eating. I have to call my dad on his cell, and sometimes I just want to go home. I don't know what it is that makes me start to worry about things, but once I get one thought in my head, the rest of the voices just start piling in and suddenly I'm upset and feeling panicky. It's like I can't breathe or something and all I can do is listen to the voices, and they scare me.

I wonder if other people have voices in their heads. I feel like such a freak sometimes. I think I'm the only kid that has problems. Everyone around me seems so normal. It's a worthless life.

I try to get through lunch hour with the hunger pains by eating three tablespoons of raw bran (the kind we use for making bran muffins at home) mixed with two teaspoons of wheat germ. I eat it dry and wash it down with lots of water so it will expand in my stomach and ease my hunger pains. Then when I'm asked later on at home if I ate lunch, I can say yes, even though I threw away the lunch that was packed for me and substituted it with bran and wheat germ. I snuck the bran and wheat germ from the pantry at home, and my parents have no clue.

January 7, 2005

After school, I take the bus home, and as soon as I get in the door, there is tension. My family is in crisis. Mealtime in our house is especially weird, because everyone is miserable. I am afraid to gain weight, so I don't eat. We never ate together before my anorexia, because often my parents were busy, so I could get away with not eating, but now that's all changed. There is a big focus on watching me eat. Mealtime causes me so much anxiety and creates chaos for everyone else. I get so bitchy. My dad and I fight over all the food I have to eat. We fight about each and every calorie, because I know it will make me fat. I negotiate everything with my dad, the serving size, and what type of food I will eat, and the calorie count of all food that enters my mouth. We yell at one another and I cry. Each mealtime begins and ends with anxiety and tears. I feel like there is a conspiracy going on. Everyone is telling me I look good, but how is that possible if I am gaining weight? They tell me my perception is distorted, but I don't know what they are talking about. I am always hungry and I am fat.

Other than mealtime, not much is going on around home. Everyone does their own thing, like homework or shopping or whatever. I spend time in my room, sometimes staring into space. Why do I have to eat anyway? Eating will make me fat. I don't want to eat and that's that. I can't seem to stop it anyway, because I am spiraling out of control. I panic whenever mealtime comes around. I wonder how come I want everything to be so perfect. I need food and I crave food and I deny myself food over and over and over again.

Nothing I do is ever good enough.

January 10, 2005

You're not going to believe this 'cause it's kind of sick. I like to cook food for other people. It's great to touch the food, and feel the food on my hands, and prepare the food, but I don't eat the food. It's really sick when you think about it. It is a way to be around food without eating it.

January 11, 2005

I read all this stuff about eating disorders at the doctor's
today. So now I am a real whacko, head case. I guess
I don't like myself very much. I often get very angry
and don't know why. I don't know what to do with my
emotions. When did I start not liking myself? When?
Anorexia is not about food. The brochure in the doctor's
office lists all the symptoms of anorexia nervosa and
anorexia bulimia. Eating disorders are psychological
disorders that manifest themselves in food.

January 13, 2005

I am an expert at vomiting. I can stick my finger down
my throat quickly and get rid of anything in my stomach.
I can walk from one room to the next and spit up in the
garbage without anyone noticing. I don't even make a
sound. Sometimes I get caught by my sister or brother,
and then they tell my parents. I am like a mouse being
hunted by the cat. My brother thinks I am off my rocker.
I yelled at him the other day for telling on me. I told him
it was not my fault that I spit in the garbage. I told him it
was the disease that made me do it. I overheard him telling
his friend how gross it was to see me puking into the
garbage can in the kitchen, and I got really sad and mad
at the same time. He thinks I am a freak, and he is telling
his friend how sick I am. It made me mad that he told,
though. He doesn't understand that the voices rule my

head. I'm not trying to be mean, but I can't help it. Why doesn't my family just leave me alone?

No one gets it. Everything keeps going in circles. First I feel awful and alone, and then when my friends try to talk to me, I want them to back off and leave me alone?????

January 15, 2005

This is really taking a toll on my dad. He looks like he has aged about seven years since he discovered I have an eating disorder. His eyes are strained and tired, and he is worried about me. He is all over me, trying to get me to eat. It's difficult for him. My dad does a great deal of work out of town, and I seem to lose the most weight when he's gone. He's worried, I can tell. I was diagnosed in October, and now in January, there is a raging, ongoing battle. Anorexia is not easy to battle.

The doctor says:

I have gained back some weight, but I am not close to being at a healthy weight. A healthy body weight for me is about 120 pounds. I am only at 110 pounds. My weight at the lowest point when I was about to have cardiac arrest was just below or at 100 pounds.

January 18, 2005

You just can't imagine how much food I have to eat to gain weight. It's ridiculous. I hate it. The worst thing is that I argue and cry and fight with my dad all the time about eating food, and I can't help it.

I go to school and come home and lay on my bed. Sometimes I read to feel better. I feel like I am the only one with these feelings, and I get very lonely in my head. When I read books, it helps, because I realize other people have troubles too. I love to read. I remember reading a book in school about South Africa called *The Power of One*. The main character was a young boy, growing up in Africa, named Pekay. He struggled with many things in his life, and he was bullied at school. Pekay described his feelings about loneliness by talking about the loneliness birds. I remembered the words, because I felt the same way. I wish the loneliness birds would come and help me. I can't remember a time when I really felt good or happy. I think about the loneliness birds when I walk to class or sit at home in my room and stare at the wall. I am still fat. I don't understand my feelings, really.

January 20, 2005

Time goes by so slowly when you feel your life is unbearable. I wonder why, day after day, I have the same stress about eating. It can't get any worse, but it hasn't gotten any better either. I am still afraid to gain weight. The exam schedule came out at school for term finals. I have four exams. My stress has increased as the pressure of exams draws nearer. Studying for exams, though, is nothing compared to the stress of mealtime. The thought of exams has sent me into a tailspin. I don't know what's worse, exams or not eating.

February 1, 2005

Well, it's all over now. Four exams in five days. Now our school starts the next term. I think I did OK.
My parents are after me all the time to eat. I'm still afraid to get fat, so I am back to my old tricks. To add insult to injury, my parents sit with me and watch me eat every morsel, as though I can't be trusted to eat on my own. It doesn't matter how much I cry or how long it takes, one of my parents sits with me 'til I eat everything. Today it took me an hour and a half to eat breakfast. I live in a fishbowl with every eyeball in the house watching me. I guess I can't be trusted. It's painful to sit at the table in the morning. I just sit and cry and cry. It doesn't help; I still have to finish the meal. Then lunch comes quickly after breakfast, because it takes me so long to eat each meal. All my time is taken up eating. I can't stand it. Calories are the enemy these days. Each bite I take makes me fatter.

February 3, 2005

My parents took the scale away. They think I only get weighed every week with the doctors, but I'm sneaky about it. I found where they hid the scale. It wasn't too difficult to find, under a plastic bin of sweaters in their second closet in the spare room.

I like to weigh myself at least ten times a day. I eat and run to the scale to see if it has changed. My parents have no clue.

The scale is my enemy today. Some days it is my friend, but today I have gained weight. The weaker my body feels from not eating, the more powerful I feel. I have power to not eat, power over food, power over my body.

February 10, 2005

I'll have to devise a new system to control my food. I'm so fat, I just can't stand how I look, and my parents are out to get me, and Dylan and Natalie are in on it too.

I think it would be easier to kill myself. I am not dead yet, but I feel such emptiness and pain. I wish someone could understand my fear of getting fat. Some people take pills or drugs or drink alcohol or jump off a building and go splat on the pavement, but I have chosen not to eat. I am afraid to eat. It's really hard to believe, but I have power over the food, and yet I'm lost and out of control. I can't remember what it felt like before, because it sure feels awful now. I'm so sad. Thoughts go back and forth in my head from one feeling to the next all the time. One minute I am OK, and the next I am panicking about something. How messed up is that?

February 11, 2005

I felt so terrible today because I overheard boys in line leaving band class discussing how a girl in my class had muscular legs like a guy. I thought, oh my God, what could they guys be saying about me if they talk about her that way. I couldn't stop thinking about it all through the next class.

February 14, 2005

Sometimes I get so angry for no reason. I mean really angry. I snap at people and say mean things. Sometimes I think that my parents just don't get it. They harp about shit like what kind of music I listen to or how I dress, but they don't get it. Why can't they see things the way I do? No one knows how I feel, and most of the time, I'm worried about just about everything in my life. My parents run around and live their lives, but don't really know what's going on in mine. They don't know how angry I get about things or how stressed out I feel when I sit in class and hear voices in my head. I wonder if the things I see are real or pretend. I just don't know.

February 15, 2005

It's been over nine months since my hellish life started spinning out of control. I don't know if it will get better. The voices in my head are quiet, but they aren't going away. They have gone from screaming to whispering. And they tell me how fat I am.

I have a regimen now. Every single day, there is a system for getting me to eat. My friends, my grandma, my aunt, my dad all meet me for lunch, and I eat with them and sit so my food digests. No more wheat germ, bran, and water. Today, I had to eat so much, I thought I would puke on the table. I had a sandwich with a slice of cheese on whole wheat, a cup of green beans, a yogurt, a plum, and a slice of homemade banana loaf, plus a glass of milk. I have put on weight and my body is nourished, but my mind still plays tricks on me. I still think I am fat. I can't get away with as much, so I am putting weight back on.

February 16, 2005

The doctor told my dad that I am out of danger of cardiac arrest. I started having hot flashes on Tuesday night before going to the doctor on Wednesday morning. The doctor said, "Hot flashes indicate the regulation of hormones in the body and the onset of menses."

February 17, 2005

I was listening to some old-fashioned music I found in the basement. There were songs like "Delilah" by Tom Jones about a woman and jealousy and a knife, and another song with lyrics about a woman, a devil woman with evil on her mind by some other band. I got to thinking about how my dad won't let me listen to certain music and even threw out some of my CDs after listening to the lyrics. He even threw out my sister's new Green Day CD that Grandma bought her at the mall. I just don't understand what is so wrong with the music; sometimes I think my dad is nuts. I don't pay attention to him anymore. He talks too much. He starts to talk and I turn off all the words. Little does my dad know that my sister, brother, and I constantly listen to the music! We listen to it after school on the Internet and TV (which we aren't supposed to have on either), and when no one is home, which is often because my parents work. We listen at our friends' houses and at school. Maybe my dad imposes the rules to pretend to other people what a great parent he is. It's all a bunch of crap and pretending. So we sneak behind his back and pretend too. I wish my life wasn't so complicated. It would be better if he didn't pretend to be concerned and make all these "good parenting rules" and we didn't have to sneak behind his back and lie about stuff like following all his rules. It would be better, I think. Maybe I think about these things too much.

I used to lie on my bed and stare at the ceiling, numb and blank. Now when I stare at the ceiling, I am trying to sort out my thoughts, and it takes up a lot of time. I try to avoid it, but the voices come back.

February 20, 2005

I don't want people to know about my eating problem, because it makes me feel bad to think people may think differently of me. I wonder what kids used to think about me. School is one of the worst places in the world, and so is my house.

February 27, 2005

School is like a blur some days. The daily activities are
like a fog. I can't remember from one minute to the next,
and my parents look at me like I am purposely forgetting,
but I am not. I just float around and forget the last thing
someone said to me. My teachers call it the teenage mind.
The eating is getting a bit better, and I am able to
concentrate better. There is less tension at home, too,
although I heard my mom on the phone with someone,
telling them about what a hellish year she is going
through. She has no clue. She lives in a fog. She took some
pictures of me just this past week so I could send them to
some modeling agencies, to see if I might model.
I snickered to myself. After all the talking at the hospital
sessions, I have learned more about anorexia and bulimia
than my mother. Modeling is the worst place in the world
for an anorexic person.
I overheard my mom's conversation on the phone, saying
how beautiful she thought I was. She is so far off the
mark, it isn't even funny. I hate myself, and feel lousy about
how I look. I mean really, what does she think about?
I can't believe she said it. I think she lives in a parallel
universe sometimes.

March 3, 2005

Going to the treatment center in the hospital and meeting
with the doctor has changed from once a week to once
every two weeks. My weight has adjusted. I am out of

danger. Instead of starving myself, I have decided to eat and vomit instead.

In French literature class today, I was gazing around the room, and all my friends were doing their assignments. I was thinking *they don't know how I feel. They don't know what it is to be fat.* None of my friends are fat. There are fat girls in the class, but they don't know how I feel either. At lunch, my friends are encouraging, and they sit and eat with me. But my skinniness startles them. They don't say so, but I scare them and make them uneasy. It's uncomfortable to talk about food at lunchtime like nothing is wrong, because it's not true. It's fake.

March 7, 2005

If I thought not eating was hard … eating is worse. I have to eat so much to gain weight. It's gross.

March 10, 2005

Didn't gain any weight this week. Thank God.

I couldn't sleep last night because all I kept thinking about was food. Eating makes me nervous. Not eating makes me nervous.

But in the morning, life goes on in the regular way with its routines, sameness. Everyone goes about their day in a regular kind of way, up for school, parents off to work.

But then I decided to change things and started to eat. I decided to eat, and now my days are chaotic. After trying and trying to control my eating, I have decided to eat. Yes.

Eat. But now that I eat, absolute panic is settling in. The food in my stomach feels like a brick. I don't want it in there.

I started to purge my food each and every time before a single calorie could be absorbed. If I throw up all the food, I can't get fat. The hard part now is to not get caught by my parents.

At first, when I was starving and little food was entering my mouth, I could puke quickly over the garbage can. But eating and puking everything up is totally different.

The first time I tried to throw up the contents of my food, it was difficult, because I had to put my entire fist in my throat to make the food come up. But I did it.

The thing now is everyone around me is being tricked because they think I am eating.

March 12, 2005

It is almost spring break. We aren't doing much. My brother Dylan might go skiing at Assissippi, and Natalie is taking a drama camp at Prairie Theatre Exchange. I haven't signed up for anything. Maybe I will be able to do a little indoor soccer practicing with my old team, now that I have gained some weight.

March 14, 2005

I am getting smarter. I am learning which foods are the right foods to eat. Foods that you can puke up easily. The trick to purging is to find the right foods to eat that can be brought up completely and totally. This way there is no trace of food to be absorbed and to make me fat.

March 17, 2005

I had dinner at Genevieve's last night. They served spaghetti. Spaghetti is a nightmare. I went to the bathroom to puke after I ate the spaghetti. The spaghetti got stuck halfway up and down my throat when I brought it up. I had to grab it and pull it the rest of the way out or bite it off, swallow the stuff in my throat again and bring it up again. From now on, spaghetti is forbidden.

We had cake for dessert. Donuts and cake are a better choice because they are much easier when they come up. They come up in a dough-like blob, and nothing is left behind in my stomach.

My friend Genevieve and her parents never suspected anything.

March 20, 2005

I am able to go shopping again with my mom to buy food. They are amazed at my turnaround about food. I have maintained my weight. When I look at the food in the cart, I am excited, because I know the food will be flushed down the toilet as soon as I eat it. I actually get excited about putting the food in the cart. I am feeling a bit smug because I wonder if anyone knows what I am doing. I look around in the grocery store to see if anyone is watching me.

March 22, 2005

One more week until spring break. I have made plans for
a few sleepovers at my girlfriend's house, a little shopping
at St. Vital Mall, and a couple of movies at the theater. My
parents are giving me some space. It amazes me that they
haven't caught me yet. It won't take them long to figure out
that my weight is not increasing.

March 23, 2005

All this vomiting is making me feel bloated and ugly. My
face is puffy, my eyes are bloodshot, and I am getting a
rash around my mouth.

I still worry about absorbing calories, so I have discovered
diuretics and laxatives that help the bloating. I searched
the Internet at school and found out about them. They
really work. I feel good when I take them, because if I
eat too much food and it makes its way to my digestive
system, the laxatives will remove the food before too many
calories get in. Another great thing is you can take them
anywhere, because they look like gum. I can take them at
school or at home or at a friend's house, so I don't have to
worry about too many calories. The pills come individually
wrapped up in a little cellophane packet like gum.

I had to steal money from my dad's bureau the other day
to buy the Ex-Lax pills. I don't think he knows, because
there was a bunch of spare change, and I am sure he didn't
count it.

March 27, 2005

Had a great time at the sleepover. Genevieve and I went to the mall and each bought a bracelet and a Roxy T-shirt. I was thinking about getting an American Eagle hoodie too, but my stomach looks awful. It is all bloating and I feel ugly. Standing in the dressing room in front of the mirror trying on the T-shirt, I noticed how far out my belly looked. I did not feel like buying the hoodie after that. I look like those kids you see on TV when World Vision is asking for money to help save the kids. I am not going to stop, though. Vomiting is the way to go.

March 30, 2005

Bloating makes me feel ugly. Puking up all the food makes me feel good. It is like a happy rush of a feeling. My brain gets numb and fuzzy, and a warm feeling creeps all over me. It doesn't last long, though. Sometimes I get a pounding headache. It turns into an ugly feeling. I won't stop, though.

April 3, 2005

Well, I have to say I have been very successful at this purging. I have control again over the food.

April 7, 2005

I knew it wouldn't last long. I had hoped it would. My dad caught on. He watched me eat all my food. Every morsel.

Then he waited and caught me puking up everything. He said he noticed I haven't lost or gained any weight, but I am eating too many calories not to gain some weight. I thought they were not paying attention, which is normally the case around here when everyone is busy, but I was wrong.

April 10, 2005

I guess I look like hell. My fingers are all swollen and red from sticking them down my throat. The stomach acid turned my fingers raw, and there are cuts on my knuckles from where my teeth rub the skin off. My hands smell too. They smell of vomit, even after I wash them. I can't get rid of the smell of puke.

April 15, 2005

I feel like a failure. No one can help me and I feel worthless. Everything goes round and round in a vicious circle. I don't know how to stop this. First I was able not to eat, and now I can't stop throwing up all the time. I can puke up to ten times a day. Sometimes I don't stop until I see blood. My stomach cramps and my muscles and diaphragm feel like they have been twisted, like when you wring out a towel.

Today, I was in the bathroom, pretending to shave my legs, and my dad asked me to leave the door open. How ridiculous. Of course I was puking again. We got in a huge

fight, and I started to cry. We are back to the open-door
policy again. They can't stop me.

April 19, 2005

We are back at the hospital group session, and now they
know I have bulimia.
The doctor asked me how this all makes me feel.
I told them that my teeth ache, my gums bleed all the time,
that I don't even taste the food anymore because I shove
it in so fast. My hair looks like straw because I am too
tired all the time and don't feel like fixing it, and my body
is bloated and shaped funny from the swelling. I told the
doctor I have no control. I used to think I could control
the binging, but I can't.
The doctor appreciated my feelings and listened to me talk
for a long time. At the end of my session, she thanked me
for sharing my feelings with her.

April 24, 2005

We sat at the kitchen table in our little nook tonight for
the first time in a long while and ate together as a family.
Dylan told us stories about what the guys were up to
at school. Jason and Michael locked a guy in his locker
because he was being a goof. We all laughed a bit tonight.
It was kind of nice for a change.

April 27, 2005

I am being tightly regulated again. My parents have set up
a scheduled routine for eating.
I guess all the retching sounds coming from the bathroom
weren't fooling my dad after all.

May 1, 2005

I am getting addicted to the laxatives. I am taking more
and more pills every day to make me feel less bloated. My
dad isn't leaving money lying around anymore, and the
laxatives are expensive. I feel bad about stealing the money
for the pills. I have to do it.

May 6, 2005

The weather is finally starting to feel like spring. The sun
is around more, and everything looks brighter. The snow
disappeared slowly this year. School seems easier these
days. I am sore from all the bloating and laxatives, but not
as tired as I was before.
At home, the mood feels better. I also am feeling less ugly.
When I feel really ugly, I vomit more and more and feel
ugly more and more.

May 9, 2005

We were all at my weekly appointment again this week.
My weight has stabilized. I am keeping some calories

down, so my weight is at 112 pounds. Everyone is happy with my weight, my parents and the doctors.

May 12, 2005

We were at my uncle's birthday party tonight, and although I didn't eat much and was watching and counting calories, I did not puke at all. I am still anxious about food, but it seems to come and go, rather than being a constant obsession in my head. My thoughts are moving around, but they aren't so dark, and the voices aren't so strong all the time.
It was a good day today.

May 14, 2005

I made the regional outdoor soccer team, which is really good, since I have not played soccer for a while now. My soccer schedule with games and practices is very busy. My dad is concerned that I eat the proper nutrition in order to maintain all the energy requirements for competitive soccer. My parents said once I stabilized my weight, I could go back to doing sports, so I am happy about that. Everything is still a negotiation, but at least I am able to play soccer now that I have more energy.

May 20, 2005

We had a home economics class today. I am taking the foods and nutrition class this session. At first, it was boring, learning how to read food labels. Then we learned to measure calories. Of course I already mastered measuring calories, so I was a great peer tutor.

I was able to help everyone do their assignment on Food Focus, the computer program. We had to calculate if the calories of the food we ate for the day matched our daily requirements to meet our energy needs. Next week, we will learn about eating disorders and body image. Today, just at the end of class, the teacher talked a bit about the media, cultural influences, and body image. There are a lot of famous young women with the same disease I have, especially models and athletes too. Next class, the teacher said she was going to read two true stories. One was written by a friend she went to school with years ago who had bulimia. Her friend was an elite athlete. The other was from a rocker magazine about this guy who was a drummer in a band, who got anorexia.

I am getting more interested in the class, because it is totally related to me. I just can't believe all the people who had anorexia too.

May 24, 2005

Nothing much to report today. I am getting better. My weekly visits to the hospital have been changed to every two weeks, and my dad isn't in my face about eating all the time.

I went to one of the school dances at lunchtime with my girlfriends, and we danced for the whole hour. It was fun.

May 28, 2005

Things at home are starting to be more normal. I am
not as anxious as I used to be about eating or about not
eating. I still worry and I look at myself in the mirror, but
I think I am getting better. I am better able to manage my
thoughts in my head. I can't say the voices are completely
gone from my head, but they are quieter. I can talk to
them and reason with them now.
Some days are worse than others, and I slip into a
panic. Other days I am fine. But I guess it is like that for
everything.

June 2, 2005

Our soccer team is going to a tournament in Minneapolis
this July, and I'm getting very excited. The place we're
playing soccer at has fifty-seven fields. Got to get through
exams first and finish grade seven.

June 8, 2005

There are tons of activities going on for the end of the
school year. I am worried about exams coming up for a
week. My aunt was over on the weekend to visit us. Since
she is a teacher, I told her I was starting to study for the
exams starting on June 15. She told me that if I learned
to be organized, and I learned to socialize, and I learned
to write a test properly, then grade seven has been a
successful year. I told her I was concentrating on the social
part the most. She told me that I was doing my job as a

student. We both laughed. She also said she was glad I
was getting better.

June 11, 2005

Our family piled in the van and went to the lake this
weekend to open up the trailer at the camp site and get
ready for summer vacation.

About The Author

Sandra Lorange was born and raised in Winnipeg,
Canada and attended the University of Manitoba. She
lives in Winnipeg with her husband and two children.
This is her first attempt at a novel.

Printed in the United States
103344LV00003B/199-690/A